SPIKEY

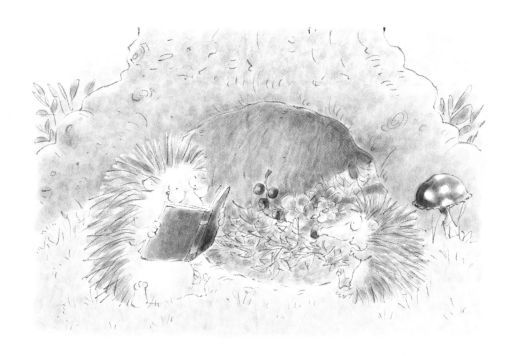

WRITTEN BY TEREZA ANTENEOVÁ

ILLUSTRATED BY MIKE PHILLIPS

For John, Taz, Gordon and all the many other very special human beings who made this book possible, with love and thanks.

Spikey © Tereza Anteneová

First Published by Compass-Publishing UK 2021
ISBN 978-1-913713-53-9

Text © Tereza Anteneová, 2021
Illustrations © Mike Phillips, 2021 (Beehive Illustration)
Tereza author photo by Ingrid Remišová

Typeset by The Book Refinery Ltd
www.thebookrefinery.com

The right of Tereza Anteneová is to be identified as the author
of this work and has been asserted by them in accordance with the Copyright,
Designs and Patents Act 1988.

A record of this book is available from the British Library catalogue.

Printed in the UK on paper from responsible sources.

This book is dedicated to all children who love animals (and to all animals who love children).

This book series is gratefully supported by Hedgehog Street in the United Kingdom

In response to the worrying decline of hedgehogs across the UK, the People's Trust for Endangered Species (PTES) and the British Hedgehog Preservation Society (BHPS) launched the Hedgehog Street campaign, which seeks to conserve this iconic species and empower the British public to help hedgehogs in people's own back gardens. By putting out some food or linking up your gardens with 'hedgehog highways', you can help hedgehogs. The PTES and BHPS are also currently commissioning various research projects into the reasons for the decline of hedgehogs and measures that could be taken to reverse the effects.

It's all about giving people an understanding of hedgehogs, why they are declining and how easy it is to help them. With their unique, charismatic and curious appearance, hedgehogs regularly feature as

'Britain's favourite wild mammal' in polls and evoke such an affectionate response from the public that there's every reason to be genuinely hopeful that we can reverse this decline.

Hedgehogs love gardens, and we know what features they need to survive and thrive in suburbia. Hedgehog Street is all about simple things everyone can do to help save our favourite wild animal. If you want to join us in the fight to save this national treasure, sign up to Hedgehog Street today at www.hedgehogstreet.org.

Throughout the book, the quiz questions on the left-hand pages are for younger readers to answer:

★ Who is Spikey?
★ Where does he live?
★ What do you think might be special about Spikey? And what do you think might be special about you?

Welcome to Spikey's World!

Hello, I am Grandma Hedgehog, and I am here to tell you about my grandson, Spikey. He is a hedgehog like I am, but to be honest with you, he is a very special hedgehog. He lives in a wonderful, big park. It might just cover the whole wide world! People call it Regent's Park, and it's in London, England. Every day, he wakes up in this park and he is excited to see where new adventures will take him.

And the questions on the right-hand pages are for older readers to answer, think about or discuss:

- What do you think it's like to live in a park?
- What do you think hedgehogs believe is important?
- Why do you think Grandma Hedgehog thinks Regent's Park is the whole wide world?

Spikey

I think being a hedgehog is pretty amazing. We have been walking around on the earth for almost 15 million years, and we have hardly changed. We are curious and slightly nosey. In fact, our noses wiggle when we smell something interesting, and we love discovering new things. We cannot see very well, but we make up for it with a good sense of hearing and an excellent sense of smell. And we are always hungry!

I am now very old for a hedgehog (over seven winters), and I have seen many, many things. My great joy in life is looking after Spikey. I love him dearly and think he's wonderful. In many ways, he is just like most other hedgehogs – handsome, with a wiggly nose, spikes and a *big* appetite – apart from one little detail. One of his back legs is thinner and shorter than the other one. It has never bothered

---

★ How does Grandma Hedgehog describe hedgehogs?
★ Which senses are the most important for hedgehogs?
★ How did the other little hedgehogs behave towards Spikey?

him, but when he was very young, his brothers and sisters and all the other little hedgehogs laughed at him because he couldn't run as fast as they could. He was so small back then that they didn't think he was a real hedgehog, and they wouldn't be friends with him.

- How do you think Spikey feels about having one leg a little shorter than the others?
- Why do you think people laugh at other people?
- What do you think Spikey did when the other hedgehogs would not play with him?

Growing up, Spikey spent lots of time talking to and learning from me, so he was never really lonely. He knew that the other young hedgehogs were bigger and stronger and faster than him. When the days became long and the air became warm, the others set off together during the night, in small groups of two and three. He asked to go with them, but they just laughed and said he could not keep up so they did not want him. They all left our cosy nest to find their own way in the world and become adult hedgehogs.

Spikey was left behind. But after lots and lots of thinking, his curious nose began to twitch, and he decided it was his turn to leave too. Each night, he looked into the darkness and tried to build up the courage to explore the world by himself. Boy, that must have been scary for him; *sooo* scary! Can you imagine how hard that decision was? So he decided

---

- ★ What did Spikey think about the other young hedgehogs?
- ★ What does Grandma Hedgehog hope Spikey will find?
- ★ How can Spiky make it easier for himself? And if you were Spikey, what questions would you ask Grandma Hedgehog?

that the night-time was still too much for him, and early one morning, he hugged me one last time and waved me goodbye. Now it is just him on his own, learning to stand on his four little feet.

I do worry about him. He left me with a twinkle in his eye and a smile in his voice, but with no other little hedgehogs to guide him. He set out into the morning light, although we hedgehogs prefer the darkness and safety of the night. I do hope he can keep out of sight and find his own way, and that his inner-hedgehog sense of right and wrong and safety and danger will guide him on his journey.

More than anything, I really hope he can find some friends, and maybe a slug, a beetle or a juicy worm or two. He's too thin.

How would you have helped Spikey if you were a baby hedgehog?

Do you think Spikey learned anything good from being left behind?

Why does Spikey leave in the morning and not at night-time? And would it be safer for Spikey to go by himself?

★ Where had Spikey been sleeping?
★ Was Spikey hungry?
★ What would you like to happen next?

Chapter One

Early one morning, Spikey woke, stretched and tasted the air. It certainly seemed like it was going to be another normal day. It had been wet all night, but now it had finally stopped raining, and the early morning sun was shining softly. The air was clean and fresh, the birds were singing, and Spikey ventured out of his cosy nest among the roots and leaves of an old tree trunk.

How would Spikey have been feeling?

Do you think Spikey liked waking up by himself?

What do you think a normal day was like for Spikey?

Spikey

Spikey wandered through the park, sniffing, his little nose pushing through the grass. He limped a little and was not very fast, but he was determined not to turn back. Spikey kept walking, and soon the sun rose and climbed up and up through the sky. He walked further and further, and the rain started up again, but this time much stronger and wilder than before.

When the clouds finally broke, the sun had started to fall towards the distant horizon, and then the shadows awoke and they too started to stretch and grow. Spikey trudged through the wet grass, and the water that had dripped down every spike onto the little hedgehog's back now soaked deep, all the way to his skin, making him feel cold.

Spikey was looking for something. He loved fruit and sweet things, especially the yummy strawberries

---

★ How far did Spikey go?
★ What does Spikey like to eat?
★ What do you think Spikey hoped would happen next?

and blueberries that he sometimes found growing wild in the park. Today, there were not many, so he thought that maybe other hedgehogs had found them first as they had wandered quietly through the night.

Spikey felt a little rumble in his tummy, and he knew he was now getting really hungry.

How would Spikey have felt when he was walking?

Were there any good things about Spikey walking by himself?

Why was Spikey sniffing, and what was he hoping to find?

★ How did Spikey feel when he heard someone crying?

★ Why was Spikey worried?

★ What do you think Spikey might say to the ladybird?

Suddenly, he heard a faint, sad noise. *Is that someone crying?* he thought. *Where is it coming from? Who can it be?*

The little sniffs made Spikey's heart sink. He did not like anyone to be unhappy, and he was worried that he may not be able to find out who was crying. So he headed in the direction of the sound, and there – between the long grasses and hiding under a big oak leaf – was a baby ladybird, looking very upset.

How would Spikey have felt when he saw the ladybird?

What problem might the ladybird have with Spikey?

What do you think the ladybird might say on seeing a hedgehog? And why do you think the ladybird might have been upset?

Spikey

"Hello, little ladybird, why are you crying?" Spikey asked softly, not wanting to scare her.

"That wild rain has made my wings really, *really* wet, and I cannot fly home." The ladybird sniffed. "Mummy and daddy will be preparing dinner, and I am not there. It's going to be dark soon, and I have never been out in the darkness all on my own before!"

"Hmmm, the park can be scary at night. I know because I'm a bit scared of it too. Maybe I can help you?" said Spikey.

The ladybird stopped crying and asked timidly, "I thought hedgehogs loved the dark? And how can you help me?"

★   How did Spikey speak to the ladybird?
★   Why was the ladybird worried?
★   What would the ladybird's parents have been thinking?

Spikey

Spikey thought there was too much to explain, so he said, "You may crawl onto my back, and I will carry you home. What do you think?"

The little ladybird looked up at the tall, sharp spikes on Spikey's back. "But you are made of great big thorns! Where can I sit so I will be safe?"

Spikey thought about this for a little while. "OK, I can see that my spikes would not be so comfy, but you may sit on my nose. It's soft and warm. What do you think?" said Spikey.

Why did Spikey want to help the ladybird?

Was it a good idea for the ladybird to trust Spikey?

What do you think the ladybird thought about sitting on Spikey's nose?

"Your nose might be soft and warm, Mr Hedgehog, but it's also just above your great big mouth!" she wailed.

What must this little ladybird think of me? Spikey wondered. *That is the question Grandma Hedgehog would certainly ask if she were here.*

Finally, he understood.

★ How did the ladybird describe Spikey's mouth?
★ How did Spikey describe himself?
★ What do you think will happen next?

"Do not worry, little ladybird," he said, "I won't harm you. I am a very friendly hedgehog and I am different from all the others. None of the other hedgehogs played with me, so I had to change the way I think and behave."

The little ladybird looked suspicious. "How did you do that?"

"Well, I am just different. Unlike all the other hedgehogs, I am now awake all day and I sleep all night. I changed my natural habits so I could find my own way in the world. I don't want to eat you, little ladybird; I want to help you, and maybe one day – if you would like it – to be your friend. Do you think you can trust me?"

How would you have felt if you were (a) the little ladybird or (b) Spikey?

Should the ladybird trust Spikey?

Why did Spikey want to be friends?

★ Why did the little ladybird stop, and what did she do?

★ How did she describe Spikey's face?

★ What was Spikey's nose doing?

Spikey

The little ladybird stopped and thought. She thought about all the stories her family had told her about the wandering giants with thorns. Then she looked at Spikey's kind face, his gentle eyes and his funny, twitching nose, and she thought about that too.

Making up her own mind, she crawled up onto Spikey's nose. "Yes, thank you," she agreed, then sniffed, with the beginnings of a smile, "I think you are a good one."

---

* What would the ladybird have been feeling?
* Do you think hedgehogs and people can change their behaviour?
* What might Grandma Hedgehog have said about Spikey offering the ladybird a lift home? And what might the ladybird's parents have said?

Spikey

Once she had settled comfortably, the little hedgehog introduced himself properly. "My name is Spikey. What's yours?" he said, making sure to keep his nose balanced and still (and almost twitch-less, which is surprisingly hard when that's all it really does).

"Well, we ladybirds don't have names like many other animals," the ladybird explained a little sadly. "I'm an insect, you see, and that means I have so many brothers and sisters that we all have very similar names. I was the ninth one to hatch, so my name is Spotty Nine. I don't like being just another Spotty, and I wish I had a special name of my own."

"My grandma said everyone should have a special name. That includes ladybirds, so you must have a name that you love." Spikey thought for a while. "How about Stripey? Do you like that?"

★ How did Spikey keep his nose still?
★ Why was the ladybird called Spotty Nine?
★ What did Grandma Hedgehog say?

Spikey

The little ladybird looked at all her beautiful, black spots and giggled. "I have spots on my back, not stripes! But it is funny and special, and I will be the only ladybird in the whole wide world called Stripey. Thank you, Spikey. I *love* it!"

How would you feel if you did not have a name? Do you like yours?

Do you think a name is important?

Why did Grandma Hedgehog think that everyone should have a special name?

★ Why was Stripey sitting on Spikey's nose?

★ How do you recognise a fox? What colours are they?

★ What might happen when the fox gets out of the hole?

Chapter Two

Spikey was glad to have made Stripey happy. He trundled along, with the little ladybird sitting on his nose and giving him directions. After a while, they came across a fox with his head far down a hole and his long tail sticking right up in the air, like a fluffy, red-and-white chimney.

How would Stripey and Spikey have felt when they saw the fox?

Have you ever made someone happy?

What would Grandma Hedgehog have said if she saw a fox?

"Hello, Mr Fox. What are you doing?" asked Spikey, completely forgetting his grandma's words of warning about foxes. "Are you playing a game?"

"I am not playing a game!" barked the fox, his voice sounding muffled from underground. "I was looking for food in this hole, and now I am stuck. Will you help me, whoever you are? I have been stuck here for three moonrises, and I am very, *very* hungry!"

"Oh dear!" exclaimed Spikey, still not realising the danger. "That is very bad luck. Let us try something."

He put the little ladybird down, and together they grabbed the fox by his tail and tried to pull him out of the hole.

"One, two, three, *heave!*" ordered Spikey.

But the fox's head remained stuck.

★ What had happened to the fox?
★ What did Spikey not realise?
★ What do you think Stripey and Spikey were expecting to happen when the fox got free?

"*Again!*" shouted Spikey. "*One, two, three, HEAVE!*"

The fox's head slowly started to appear, but they could see his ears had now become stuck.

"*Try to wiggle your ears, Mr Fox!*" shouted Stripey.

Then Spikey called, "One last time; *one, two, three, HEEEEAVE!*"

Finally, with a wiggle and a jiggle and a slight pop, the fox's head jerked back out of the hole.

How did you feel when Stripey and Spikey met the fox?

Is it always good to help?

What do you think Spikey might have done when he saw the fox if he hadn't been with Stripey?

★ What did the fox want to do to Stripey and Spikey, and why?

★ What had Grandma Hedgehog said about foxes?

★ What did Spikey have to do quickly?

Chapter Three

They all lay panting on the grass. Uncorking foxes is hard work!

The fox cast his eyes around and then looked slyly at Spikey. "Well, that was very…convenient," said the fox, "I see you are a tasty little hedgehog, so I am going to eat you because I am *sooo* hungry. And I can eat this soggy ladybird too, for my dessert!"

Spikey started to tremble because, at that moment, he remembered what his grandma had told him: "Beware of foxes. They can easily chew you up!" But it was too late now, and he had to think quickly.

✎ How did you feel when the fox was speaking? And how do you think Stripey and Spikey would have been feeling?

✎ Was the fox fair in his thinking?

✎ Have you ever had to think quickly?

Spikey

"Well, Mr Fox, we helped you," said Spikey, trying to sound like a parent fox, which is not easy to do when you look like a hedgehog. "Yes, you can eat us. Or…or…or you could be our friend and help us!" Spikey was speaking with a new-found bravery he never knew he had. "I eat insects, but I am helping my new friend – Stripey – to get home, because her wings are too wet to fly. Please, Mr Fox, will you think again? Instead of eating us, would you help get this little ladybird home safely?"

★ Who did Spikey try to sound like?
★ What did Stripey say to the fox?
★ Why was Spikey helping the fox?

"Why would I do that?" asked the fox, surprised by the courage of the little hedgehog, who reminded him of his father (which he found very confusing).

"Because we have just helped you get your fat head out of that hole, and now we deserve to be your friends and not your supper," said Stripey.

How did you feel when you heard Spikey speak? And how would the fox have felt?

Were Stripey and Spikey right to expect the fox to be friendly?

What was Spikey trying to do?

Spikey

The fox paused. Something inside him was pulling his thinking in two different directions. Then his stomach let out a long, hollow growl all by itself.

Stripey tugged at Spikey's spikes and whispered, "Let's go...now!"

Spikey waited, feeling confused. *I imagined Mr Fox would be happy to be freed from that hole*, he thought, but then he saw the flash of the fox's eyes and his long, sharp teeth.

Finally, his hedgehog sense took over. "Stripey, hang on! I'm curling. I'm curling!" And with that, the little hedgehog rolled himself into the very tightest ball he could. It was just in time, as he felt the snap of the fox's jaws around him.

★   Why did the fox's tummy make a noise?
★   What did Spikey do?
★   How did the fox's face change?

How did you feel when the fox's tummy made a noise?

Was it right for Stripey and Spikey to think the fox would change?

Why were the fox's feelings being pulled in two different directions?

"*Owww!*" shouted Spikey.

"*Owww!*" howled the fox.

"*Owww!*" squeaked Stripey as she jumped from spike to spike and away from those snapping jaws. "*Wings, wings!*" she shouted, but they were still too weak after getting so wet.

Snap, snap, snap!

"*Owww, owww, owww,*" all three owwwed.

"*We can't stay here,*" shouted Stripey. "*You need to roll!*"

"Where to?" cried Spikey, feeling more and more scared. He wished his grandma and every hedgehog in the world were here to help him, but he wasn't alone now.

"*Follow my orders!*" shouted Stripey, "*There's a fence over there by the park-keeper's hut. It has a hole in it. Let's go! Forwards and to the left. Go, go, go!*"

Snap!

★   What was wrong with Stripey's wings?
★   What was Spikey trying to do?
★   Do you think Spikey will roll in the right direction?

Spikey

"*Owww, owww, owww!*" wailed Stripey.

"What does 'left' mean?" cried Spikey.

"*Your funny-leg side!*" shouted Stripey, forgetting to be polite.

Snap!

"Owww, owww, owww," Stripey whimpered.

Now Spikey understood which way to go. He was lucky to have different legs. What would he have done if they were all the same?

What did you think when Stripey shouted about Spikey's funny leg?

How do you know when something will help?

What would have happened to Spikey if Stripey had not been there?

Spikey

Snap!

"*Owww, owww, owww!*" howled Spikey and Stripey in unison. There was no time to think about his different leg now. Spikey began to roll forwards and to the left.

"*You're doing it, Spikey! You're going forwards and to the left!*" shouted Stripey, jumping up and down among the spikes herself. She was trying to avoid those snapping jaws and also see where they needed to go. It was *hard*.

Snap!

"*Owww, owww, owww!*" Spikey and Stripey exclaimed together again.

"Keep rolling, Spikey! You're doing *sooo* well. And now to the right!" cried Stripey.

"What does 'right' mean?" squeaked Spikey, starting to panic.

★ How was Spikey picking the correct direction?
★ What was Stripey doing?
★ Why was the fox getting weaker?

"*Not left!*" yelled Stripey, finding it really hard to hang on. She had never driven a hedgehog before. It was *not* easy.

Spikey understood what she meant: his other-leg side. Snap!

"*Owww, owww, owww!*" they both cried once more.

They were rolling and rolling towards the fence, but Spikey was getting tired. And he hurt. Stripey was getting tired too, and she hurt from both all the jumping around on Spikey's sharp spikes and avoiding the fox's frightening, sharp teeth. Even the fox was getting tired. He had not eaten for days, he was growing weaker and weaker, and this was such a sharp hedgehog!

Suddenly, everything changed. All three found themselves facing another danger. Something bigger and much, *much* worse. And it was right in front of them!

- What saved Spikey when he was panicking and in trouble?
- Do we always know what will help us?
- Who is the hero right now?

★   Why did everyone stop moving?

★   Why were Spikey and the fox tired?

★   How big was the hound?

Spikey was so scared that he just stopped rolling. He couldn't move any further forwards, no matter how hard he tried. He just froze. The fox froze too. He was very tired and very sore, and he could barely move. Hunger and pain had finally caught up with him, and now he was looking straight up into the eyes of danger.

Just in front of them, there was a hound who belonged to the park-keeper – and he was *very* big!

---

* How did the fox feel? And how did Stripey and Spikey feel?
* How did the fox, Stripey and Spikey end up in this situation?
* What might the hound have been thinking? Do you think the hound might make friends with Spikey, Stripey and the fox?

Chapter Four

"Well, well, well! A tired little fox," the hound growled. "I don't like foxes. I don't make friends with foxes. I only talk to foxes before they meet their end. And I am their end."

Everything went very still.

Spikey peeped up. He could see the terrified fox lying flat on the ground, panting and shaking. He could also see the hound, fierce and strong, staring down at the cowering fox.

The fox closed his eyes and whispered, "Please make it quick, Mr Hound."

The hound barked, snapped and leaped forwards, his jaws open wide.

"*Nooo!*" Stripey cried out.

★   Who was the hound speaking to?

★   Did the hound notice Stripey and Spikey?

★   How did the fox behave?

Spikey

Something deep inside Spikey awoke. Something that was not hedgehog and not Spikey, but something else. A feeling of anger. Even though the fox was their enemy, Spikey couldn't stand by and watch him being hurt. He had to do something! Spikey rolled into a ball and threw himself in front of the snarling hound.

The dog was so busy attacking the fox that he did not even notice the small, sharp ball of spikes approaching. His soft, wet and *very* sensitive nose was not expecting to meet a rolling Spikey, and before he knew it, his nose was deep in the little hedgehog!

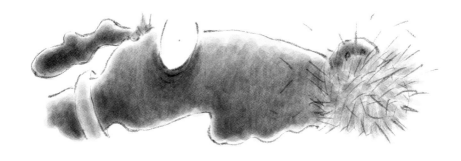

How would the fox have been feeling? And why was Spikey angry?

Was Spikey right to help the fox?

What was Spikey hoping to do? Do you think it will work?

"*OOOOOOOOOOOOWWWWWWWWWWW!*"
howled the dog – much, *much* louder than any
'owww' Regent's Park had ever heard before. He
leaped backwards and shook his throbbing nose,
hedgehog and all, as hard as he could, flinging
Spikey off his snout. Then he raced off with his tail
between his legs.

★   How loud did the hound howl?
★   Why did the hound have his tail between his legs?
★   Where was Spikey now?

How did you feel when Spikey helped the fox?

What would you do now if you were the fox?

Do you think the fox learned something?

Spikey

As he flew up into the sky, Spikey could see the dog disappearing into the distance. For a brief moment, he thought being in the air was really good for looking around.

Stripey looked up at him excitedly. *"You're flying! You're flying!"* she shouted.

But then Spikey dropped like a stone and landed by the fence. *Splash!* He came down in the hound's water bowl, which broke his fall and meant he was unhurt but wet. Stripey hurried over to him, and – looking very sheepish – the fox crawled slowly towards them.

"Thank you...thank you," he whispered. "You saved me."

★   What happened to the hound?
★   Can Spikey fly?
★   What happened to Spikey?

How would the fox have felt when he was helped by Spikey?

What would you do now if you were Spikey?

What happened when Spikey was 'flying'?

Chapter Five

Stripey looked coldly at the fox. She did not trust him one little bit. "So what now, *Foxface*? Hedgehog and ladybird sandwiches?"

The fox dropped his head. "I'm sorry, little ladybird, but I am a fox, and a very hungry one. It's my nature to eat hedgehogs and insects. But I never realised how frightening being eaten is until the moment I met that hound. I will not eat you, I promise. I will lie here and sleep one last time. Please go. I am sorry. I am so, *so* sorry."

The grass started to rustle, and a wet, black nose poked through it, twitching. "Mr Fox, I know it is in your nature, but we helped you. Twice," Spikey said gently. "And we will help you again. Follow me...or

---

★   What do foxes eat?

★   How many times have Stripey and Spikey helped the fox so far?

★   What did Stripey call the fox?

follow your nose…There's something for you only a few paw-lengths away."

The fox shook his nose and followed the smell of soggy hedgehog. There was nothing else he could do. He crawled very, *very* slowly.

As Spikey promised, not far away was the dog's bowl. "I landed in this," said Spikey, pointing towards it. "I was lucky; it's full of water. The one just behind it…is full of…I don't know what it is, but it's very smelly and tastes really, *really* nice, so you might like it. I tried a little bit while you were chatting to Stripey. I can still smell the hound on it, though."

The fox looked up. His nose was not working properly after being prickled with so many hedgehog spikes, but he caught just the slightest, slightest, *slightest* whiff of dog food. He used the last of his energy to crawl to the food and slowly began to eat.

---

* Do you feel we should trust the fox?
* When would you help someone who had not helped you?
* What had the fox learned this time round?

Within a few mouthfuls, he could feel his energy and power starting to return. He soon finished almost everything, but not quite.

"Little hedgehog, thank you. You saved me! Once in the hole, once with that hound and once again with this meal. Why did you help me? I don't understand it. I wasn't nice to you," stated the fox.

Spikey thought for a while. "We helped you the first time because you needed help. We helped you the second time because you needed more help, and Stripey and I knew that, whatever happened, we still wanted to help. And we helped you again just now as you needed help so badly. Are you going to eat us now?"

★ Did Stripey trust the fox?
★ What is wrong with the fox's nose?
★ Why was Spikey soggy?

The fox was still very hungry, but he had learned something important. "Of course not, little hedgehog. I will not eat you or your ladybird friend. Not now. Not ever. I promise a 'fox promise'. I will help you both whenever I can, in my own way. I have left some food for you, if you would like it?"

Was Spikey right to help the fox a third time?

Why would Spikey have nibbled some of the dog food while the fox was so weak?

What do you think a 'fox promise' is?

Spikey looked deep into the fox's tired eyes. Something in his hedgehog senses warned him, but something deeper still knew he could trust the fox. Spikey stepped forwards and soon – with a snuffle, a slurp and a grunt (hedgehogs are not polite eaters) – finished off the food. "That was amazing," said Spikey. "Almost as good as blueberries!"

"And…eeerrrm…what about me? I'm hungry too!" said Stripey, three of her feet tapping the ground until she felt wobbly.

The fox looked at the ladybird and thought, *What do ladybirds eat?* He couldn't imagine her tucking into a rabbit or a mouse. *Ladybird food? That is a very hard question.* "What do ladybirds eat, little one?" he asked finally.

"*Aphids!*" she shouted back, "*Bring me AAAAPPPPPHHHHHHIIIIIIIIIIIIIIIDDDDDDSSSSSSSS!*"

★   What were Spikey's hedgehog senses doing?
★   Had everybody eaten or was someone still hungry?
★   Why is one bowl yellow and one bowl red?

How do you feel about Spikey, Stripey and the fox now?

Should Spikey trust his hedgehog senses?

Do you think foxes or people can change their nature?

"What are aphids?" asked the fox.

"Aphids?" gasped Stripey, amazed that not everyone had heard of them. "Aphids are green or black little bundles of tasty ladybird food. They are fat and juicy, and their little legs wiggle when you munch them. Do you have any?"

The fox thought that this was exactly how ladybirds behaved when he munched them, but he did not say anything. "I promised to help, and a fox is only as good as his fox promise," he said. "Where do you live, little ladybird?"

"Close to the Rose Garden on the other side of the park," answered Stripey, both antennae aloft and slightly to the left. "Aphids eat roses, so ladybirds really like to be near roses too!"

Spikey had never heard of the Rose Garden, and it sounded far away. "Will you help us get there?"

★ What does Stripey want and why?
★ What does the fox remember as being 'fat and juicy' with wiggling legs?
★ Where is the Rose Garden?

asked Spikey, "This little ladybird is already late home, and I do not know the way."

"Climb onto my back and hold tight," the fox ordered. "We'll be there before sunset tonight."

---

* Why was Stripey shouting?
* What might an aphid think of this conversation?
* Would Stripey and Spikey want to crawl onto the fox's back?

Spikey

Spikey helped Stripey up onto his nose, and, in turn, the fox helped the two of them onto his back, carefully avoiding the sharp spikes. His nose and paws still hurt, and he did not want to meet any more hedgehog spikes today.

★ How did Stripey and Spikey get onto the fox's back?
★ What was the fox trying to do?
★ Do you think Stripey and Spikey would enjoy the ride?

- How did the fox feel?
- Can Stripey and Spikey trust the fox now?
- (a) Can these three be friends? (b) What does friendship mean to you?

Chapter Six

As they walked together through the park, the fox's two passengers felt like having a friendly chat.

"What is your name?" asked Spikey, trying to get comfortable.

"I don't think I have a name," replied the fox, "If I do, I can't remember it. It has been *sooo* long since anyone talked to me, as everybody is so scared of me that they just run away."

"All of our friends should have a real name," said Spikey. "How about White Tip?"

Stripey looked puzzled. "Why not 'Fangs'…or 'Jaws'…or 'Sore Nose'…or 'Smells Like Fox'?" Then she spotted his tail. "I get it! His tail. His tail is white at the tip!"

"I *love* White Tip," agreed the fox.

★ How long had it been since anyone had spoken to the fox?
★ What would you have suggested as the fox's name?
★ What was White Tip doing during the journey?

Spikey

White Tip felt proud to have a real name and he set off with his head held high.

He raced across the park, leaping over stones, around trees, through wide stretches of water and along secret paths. He almost asked them to keep a lookout for the hound, but he felt they'd had enough troubles for one day, so he did not ask. He kept a careful lookout, though, but Stripey and Spikey didn't know this. They just saw the park flashing by, and they felt the wind whistle around them as they hung on excitedly.

- Why did Stripey suggest the fox names that she did?
- Why is what we call ourselves important? Does this mean that people should be able to choose their own names?
- Why did White Tip not ask them to look out for the hound? Was this a good decision?

★   What plants do you think grow in the Rose Garden?

★   Why was Stripey being dangerous?

★   Why is Stripey able to fly now?

Spikey

As the green grass passed under White Tip's paws, Stripey shouted, *"Look! I can see the Rose Garden now!"*

White Tip slowed to a gentle run, and he came to a halt just beside the beautiful display of roses.

Stripey lifted her tiny shell and extended her wings. The evening air flowed smoothly over each one as they spread out and clicked neatly into place. "Oh yes! Look! Look! Look! My wings are dry, and I can fly again and get home in time for dinner. Yippeee!" She lifted off and started turning happy, red somersaults above their heads. "So aphids beware! There is a dangerous and very hungry ladybird on the loose!"

Why was Stripey turning somersaults in the air?

Where is truly home to Stripey?

Why do you think it is important to be home in time for dinner?

"Well, it looks like you can get home all on your own now," said Spikey to the little ladybird, a little sadly. "We cannot come with you because your mummy and daddy might be scared of White Tip and me."

★ What does Stripey want to do?
★ Why can't Spikey and White Tip accompany Stripey home?
★ What is a somersault?

"Yes, that's true, but I have had so much fun with you both! Shall we meet again tomorrow? Where can I find you?" asked Stripey.

"I don't really have a home, so I will curl up and sleep nearby," explained Spikey. "Don't worry, you will always find me. Remember, I am not that quick," he added with a smile, as he thought about where his home really was.

"How about you, White Tip?" Stripey wanted to know.

"Thank you, my friends. But a fox needs to wander and explore the night. You may not always see me, but I will always be nearby," said White Tip with a wink. "Whenever you need me, call my new name. Only you two know of it."

The little ladybird waved them goodbye and did a few more somersaults in the air, just because she could.

---

* Why did Stripey say she'd had fun?
* Where is truly home to Spikey?
* (a) Why did Spikey want to curl up and sleep? (b) What do you think White Tip might do now?

Spikey

Spikey watched Stripey fly excitedly towards a crack in the wall of a cottage near the Rose Garden. She flew into it and, a moment or two later, flew out again with her mother. They looked happy to be together again. He watched them heading back to the Rose Garden for a feed. Some of the roses were covered with aphids, and Stripey set off for her supper with a shout of joy.

Spikey and White Tip envied her – they were both still very hungry – until they spotted a bush of ripe blueberries growing wild in the garden. They soon ate their fill, with the sweet juice staining their faces.

★ Who does Stripey fly to the Rose Garden with? Why?
★ What did Spikey hope?
★ Why did Spikey and White Tip have blue lips?

Spikey

A little later, Stripey and her mother flew back high over White Tip and Spikey, who both looked so small to Stripey just then, and she could see the mess they had made in the garden. She looked down at them with a grin. "You two must be the first animals in the world with blue lips!" she said with a giggle.

Soon after he had finished his (very large!) feast, Spikey looked around for White Tip, but the fox had already slipped quietly away. There was no sign of him, and Spikey knew the fox had set off into the night. He just hoped there were no other hounds waiting to trouble his new friend.

How would Spikey have felt when Stripey and White Tip left?

Why did White Tip leave so quietly without saying goodbye?

Why did Spikey and White Tip look so small to Stripey at the end?

Spikey

Spikey found himself a deep hole nearby that was full of leaves, and he knew he'd found a secret hedgehog nest built by other hedgehogs long ago. He checked it was safe, snuggled down into it and thought about his day. That morning, he had been cold, wet and hungry, and with no friends around. Tonight, he was warm, dry and full, and he had two new friends. It was a wonderful feeling, and he felt himself drifting off to sleep, knowing he was safe and happy and ready for a new day tomorrow.

★ Where did Spikey sleep?
★ What had Spikey's day been like?
★ What do you think will happen to Spikey, Stripey and White Tip tomorrow?

- How would Spikey have been feeling?
- Why was it so important to Spikey to have two friends?
- What did Spikey, Stripey and White Tip learn on their journey? And what did you learn on your journey with Spikey, Stripey and White Tip?

If you enjoyed answering the questions at the bottom of the pages, you can find more on Spikey's own website. It also has lots of facts about hedgehogs, which are truly amazing. Visit www.thelittlehedgehog.com.

Further information about hedgehogs and how to help them can be found by visiting the Hedgehog Street website given at the beginning of the book or by contacting the British Hedgehog Preservation Society at www.britishhedgehogs.org.uk.

About the Author

Tereza Anteneová

As a girl, Tereza lived in a small village just outside one of the castles of Prague, Czechoslovakia (now in the Czech Republic), next to an old wood and a gentle, flowing stream. She and her father spent long summer days lying in the grass, watching the wildlife, and telling each other stories about the lives, hopes and dreams of all the animals they saw. Soon, the world of Spikey and all his friends was born.

Later, Tereza and her family moved to England, and after a few years, she missed Spikey and his friends, so they all moved back to the Czech Republic again.

Tereza grew up. She worked hard, and Tereza became a journalist, a newsreader and a political reporter, allowing her to tell different stories to the whole wide world.

But she missed Britain, so she moved back to England again. Tereza now lives in Islington, London, with her fiancé John and their two cats, Meowglish and Johnson. But her heart still lies with Spikey and his friends, beside that little stream and the gentle world that Tereza and her father created so long ago.